High Mountains

Starlight Caves

Rainbow Pools

Huts

Ice Owls

Burning Bushes

Lake

Sledging Slopes

Gardens

School

Kennels

Ridge

Husky Training Ground

Fields

LAND OF ICE AND WINTER

Linda Chapman lives in Leicestershire with her family and two dogs. When she is not writing, she spends her time looking after her three children, reading, talking to people about writing, and horse riding whenever she can.

You can find out more about Linda on her websites at *lindachapman.co.uk* and *lindachapmanauthor.co.uk*

Books by Linda Chapman

BRIGHT LIGHTS

CENTRE STAGE

MY SECRET UNICORN series

NOT QUITE A MERMAID series

SKATING SCHOOL series

SKY HORSES series

STARDUST series

UNICORN SCHOOL series

Skating School

Amber Skate Star

Linda Chapman

Illustrated by Nellie Ryan

PUFFIN

Madame Letsworth's Magic Ice-Skating Academy

ICE OWLS

ISSY JO MAISIE MILLY

With special thanks to Lee Weatherly

PUFFIN BOOKS

Published by the Penguin Group
Penguin Books Ltd, 80 Strand, London WC2R ORL, England
Penguin Group (USA) Inc., 375 Hudson Street, New York, New York 10014, USA
Penguin Group (Canada), 90 Eglinton Avenue East, Suite 700, Toronto, Ontario, Canada M4P 2Y3
(a division of Pearson Penguin Canada Inc.)
Penguin Ireland, 25 St Stephen's Green, Dublin 2, Ireland (a division of Penguin Books Ltd)
Penguin Group (Australia), 250 Camberwell Road, Camberwell, Victoria 3124, Australia
(a division of Pearson Australia Group Pty Ltd)
Penguin Books India Pvt Ltd, 11 Community Centre, Panchsheel Park, New Delhi – 110 017, India
Penguin Group (NZ), 67 Apollo Drive, Rosedale, North Shore 0632, New Zealand
(a division of Pearson New Zealand Ltd)
Penguin Books (South Africa) (Pty) Ltd, 24 Sturdee Avenue, Rosebank, Johannesburg 2196, South Africa

Penguin Books Ltd, Registered Offices: 80 Strand, London WC2R ORL, England

puffinbooks.com

First published 2010
1

Text copyright © Linda Chapman, 2010
Illustrations copyright © Nellie Ryan, 2010
All rights reserved

The moral right of the author and illustrator has been asserted

Set in 15/22 pt Bembo
Typeset by Palimpsest Book Production Limited, Grangemouth, Stirlingshire
Made and printed in England by Clays Ltd, St Ives plc

British Library Cataloguing in Publication Data
A CIP catalogue record for this book is available from the British Library

ISBN: 978-0-141-33080-8

www.greenpenguin.co.uk

Penguin Books is committed to a sustainable future
for our business, our readers and our planet.
The book in your hands is made from paper
certified by the Forest Stewardship Council.

Contents

In the Magic Land of
Ice and Winter . . .

In the staffroom at the Magic Ice-skating
Academy, Madame Letsworth, the
headteacher, was sipping a cup of fragrant
tea. Her heart was heavy. Outside, in the ice
sylphs' world, the snow on the trees was
glistening as it very gradually began to melt.

Madame Li, one of the other teachers,
gazed out of the window. 'It's getting
warmer,' she said, sighing.

Madame Letsworth nodded. Every hundred years in the Land of Ice and Winter, an Ice Princess had to be found to perform the Dance of Winter – an ice dance that kept the land frozen. But finding the Ice Princess wasn't easy. She had to be a human girl with very special qualities, as well as a love of ice-skating deep in her heart.

Madame Letsworth thought of the twelve girls who had arrived at the Academy the week before by magic. Hopefully one of them would become the new Ice Princess in five weeks' time . . . but which one?

She joined Madame Li at the window. 'Our Ice Princess will need to be very brave,' she murmured, staring out at their beautiful, sparkling world. 'The Ice Caves will be tricky – and dangerous.'

In the Magic Land of Ice and Winter . . .

Madame Li's face turned solemn at the mention of the caves. She nodded. 'This week's competition will help us decide,' she replied.

Chapter One
Skating School

Issy Roberts stirred as she felt a faint fluttering on her cheek. Opening her eyes, she grinned. Cobweb, the tiny frost fairy, was tickling her face.

'Hello, Cobweb.' Sitting up in bed, Issy flicked her heavy blonde fringe out of her eyes and looked around her at the Ice Owls dorm. She had been at the Magic Ice-skating Academy for over a week now, but every morning when she woke up, she half expected to find herself back in her bed at home. She could still hardly believe that she was really in a magical land. Things like this weren't supposed to happen in real life!

Cobweb squeaked a polite reply and then flew off with the other frost fairies to get the girls' clothes ready.

'Here, let me help you,' said Issy, jumping out of bed. The frost fairies found it difficult to do their work on warmer days because their magic was weaker and Issy liked to help them whenever she could.

'Oh, here we go again,' groaned her friend Jo from across the dorm. The tall, brown-haired girl sat up in bed with a wicked gleam in her eye. 'Looking after the fairies. You'll be starting a frost fairy fan club next – I'm surprised Sophy hasn't already!'

Issy flushed. Sophy, from the Snow Foxes dorm, was her best friend at the Academy, but Jo didn't like her much. They were just so different – Sophy was quiet and thoughtful and into magic whereas Jo was forever teasing people and getting into trouble.

'Oh, Sophy and I aren't starting a frost fairy fan club,' Issy said, smiling at Jo and trying to make a joke out of it. 'But we might start an ice dragon one instead!'

'Ha, ha, very funny,' said Jo, jumping out of bed. 'We should call you two the Fairy Friends.' She flapped her arms as if they were wings. 'You could even dress up as them – I bet that's just the sort of thing Sophy would like to do! You could wear wings and little dresses and . . .'

'Oh, stop going on, Jo,' giggled Maisie, running a comb through her curly black hair.

Her twin sister Milly nodded. She and Maisie shared the Ice Owls dorm too. They looked almost exactly alike, except that Milly had longer, braided hair and darker eyes. 'There's nothing wrong with liking the frost fairies,' said Milly. 'I think they're sort of cute.'

'What!' said Jo in pretend outrage. 'Those little wasp-things? You've got to be – *mmph*!' She broke off abruptly as Issy threw a pillow that hit her in the face. With a laugh, she hurled the pillow back. 'Oy!'

'You're lucky they don't put icicles in your bed,' said Issy, only half joking as she glanced at the fairies, who were darting around the room. She hoped their feelings hadn't been hurt. '*I* would, if I were them.'

'They know I'm only teasing,' said Jo breezily.

Issy shook her head and smiled. She hoped the frost fairies did know that most of the time Jo *was* just messing around.

As she got dressed, Maisie started singing
a pop song that they all knew. The frost
fairies fluttered about in time to the music.

'Ooh, I love this one!' cried Jo. She
grabbed Issy's hands. 'Come on, Is – let's
show these fairies how to *really* move!'

Issy threw herself into the dance,
shrieking with laughter as the two of them
twirled and spun each other round the
room.

★

9

That morning the girls had a lesson with
Madame Longley, the grey-haired ice sylph
who taught them about the Land of Ice and
Winter, and then afterwards they had a
free-skating session. Issy hurried down to
the rink. As much as she loved learning
about the land, ice-skating was even better.
She loved skating more than anything!

As Issy went through the double doors,
she spotted Sophy standing to one side of
the rink, peering inside one of the large
purple music boxes. Issy waved then put
on her skates and stepped on to the ice.

Jo zoomed up to her, stopping in a spray
of ice crystals. 'Hi, Is! Come and play tag!'

'Um . . . not right now.' Issy glanced in
Sophy's direction and smiled.

'Oh, I see,' said Jo, following her gaze
'You're going to skate with *her*.'

'Jo . . .' But Jo had already skated off to ask Maisie to play tag with her instead.

Sighing, and wishing her friends could just get on, Issy skimmed across the ice to Sophy.

'Hi!' Sophy greeted her. She was small with dark-brown hair and sparkling hazel eyes. Like Issy, she wore a simple skating dress, tights and a wrap-over cardigan. She was holding up the lid of the music box.

'What are you doing?' Issy asked her, pushing away thoughts of Jo.

'I thought the ice dragons might like a bit of that sticky toffee pudding we had for dessert,' said Sophy.

Issy peered into the box. The pale-blue ice dragons inside the box made the music play for the girls' skating routines by turning a complicated system of wheels and levers. Issy loved them, but it had never occurred to her to feed them pudding! She giggled as she watched them devour the treat Sophy had saved for them, smacking their lips enthusiastically. Their paws and mouths looked very sticky!

Sophy fed the last of the pudding to the dragons. 'Come on then! Let's skate!'

They did their stretches together and

then did a lap round the rink, chatting about the class they'd just had with Madame Longley. She had been telling them about some of the plants in the magic land – amazing bushes that burnt with a golden icy-cold fire; silvery arctic creepers that hung from the trees and were almost invisible until you got tangled up in them; and rainbow berries that changed colour every week. She had also told them more about the wild ice dragons who lived in the woods nearby. Their eggs had hatched not long ago, and in a few days the baby ice dragons would begin learning how to fly.

'I'd love to see one,' said Issy as she and Sophy glided round a curve. 'Can you imagine how tiny they are?'

'Like little baby mice!' exclaimed Sophy.

'They must be *so* sweet – we'll have to go and see if we can find some soon.'

The rink was a whirlwind of activity, with some girls skating backwards and others skating forwards, some performing spirals and others jumping. Issy watched Jo throw herself into a double toe loop and wasn't surprised to see her wobble on the landing. Jo loved skating, but she didn't always have the patience to practise her footwork! Milly, who was in the advanced group, was the exact opposite. She worked hard on everything, and skated with great grace and skill.

And then there was Cecilia! Issy grinned. 'Look,' she said, nudging Sophy.

Sophy stifled a laugh. Cecilia, a very pretty beginner skater who was in the Snow Foxes dorm, had stopped at the side

of the rink to refasten her thick chestnut
ponytail. A small swarm of frost fairies
hovered nearby, holding up a mirror. 'Oh,
this icy air!' Issy heard her exclaim
anxiously as she and Sophy skated past. 'It
makes my hair go all frizzy.'

Issy and Sophy exchanged amused looks
once they were past. '*Oh, this icy air!*'
mimicked Issy softly and they both
giggled.

'We shouldn't laugh at her really,' said

Sophy quickly. 'I know she's silly about her looks, but if she could just forget how pretty she is, she'd be really nice. She's always happy to lend things to people – and she can be really good fun.'

They separated to practise on their own. As always, once Issy was whizzing about on the ice, the rest of the world seemed to fade away. She loved skating fast and doing jumps, and although she fell over a lot, the feeling she got when she landed a jump perfectly made all the bruises worthwhile.

I'll do a double lutz, she thought. Going into backward crossovers, she went faster and faster. Shifting her weight to her left foot, she touched her right toe pick to the ice and sprang into the air, rotating her shoulders. Two turns and then she landed neatly, throwing her arms out into a glide.

Yes! Issy thought triumphantly. Her lessons at the Academy were already paying off. Just last week, she'd had trouble with that jump.

Vanessa, a sour-faced girl with long, dark-blonde hair, had been watching with a smirk. 'Of course, if you were *really* any good, Issy, you'd be doing double axels by now. When Mummy and Daddy took me to the Olympics, a coach there watched me skate and *he* said –'

Issy ignored her and skated on until she was out of earshot. Vanessa was always boasting about how good she was at skating, but she was only in the intermediate group – much to her disgust! *Maybe I* will *try a double axel*, Issy thought. *Why not?* She knew she'd probably just tumble on to the ice as usual, but so what?

She picked up speed. *Now!* she thought. Leaning on to the forward outside edge of her left foot, she shot up and spun in the air twice. When she came to land, her right foot wavered and she almost fell. Still, that was much better than she usually did! She really *was* improving. Issy practised the double axel over and over again, becoming more and more confident with each jump. Sometimes she *did* fall, but she just brushed herself off and tried again.

Suddenly Issy heard a whistle blow. Looking up, she saw Madame Letsworth, the headteacher and advanced ice-skating coach, standing beside the rink in her dark-maroon dress.

'That's enough for now, girls,' she called.

'Go and get changed, and then come to the hall. It's time for me to tell you about this week's competition!'

Chapter Two
Exciting News

The girls rushed off the ice to the changing area. Sophy looked at Issy in excitement. 'What do you think this week's competition will be?'

'I don't know,' Issy replied. 'But I can't wait to find out!'

At the end of every week at the Academy there was a competition designed to help the teachers decide who the Ice Princess would be. Last week's competition had been to perform a routine that showed the girls' personalities on the ice. Sophy had been the winner and had been awarded a gorgeous pair of sapphire skates.

Issy had been very pleased for her best friend, who had worked hard. She'd love to have a pair of jewelled skates herself though. *Maybe* I'll *be the winner this week*, she thought hopefully as she got changed.

'I wonder what sort of skates we'll have for a prize this time?' mused Jo.

'Maybe diamonds!' burst out Maisie. '*Diamonds are a girl's best friend*,' she sang, holding her hairbrush like a microphone. Everyone laughed.

'Well, *I* want to know more about the
Ice Princess and what she has to do,' said
Abigail from the Frost Fairies dorm.
'They've hardly told us anything and I'm
sooo curious!'

There was a chorus of agreement. All
the girls wanted to know more. They
knew the land was melting and that the Ice

Princess would have to do a dance to stop that happening, but they didn't know anything else.

It's so beautiful here, Issy thought as she pulled a sweater on over her jeans. *I hope I get to be the Ice Princess so that I can help*.

Soon all the girls were gathered in the hall. Madame Letsworth smiled at them. 'I'm sure you're all eager to hear about the competition. Well, this week, the other teachers and I would like you to do an ice-skating routine that shows bravery.'

Bravery? Issy felt a tingle go through her as the girls looked at each other in surprise.

Madame Letsworth continued. 'Without being silly or taking risks, we want you all to push yourselves to do that little bit extra this week and try things in your routine that you wouldn't normally do. Confront your fears!'

Issy blinked. She wasn't sure that she *had* any fears when it came to skating. She loved doing it so much that it had never occurred to her to be afraid! But pushing herself to do new things sounded great.

Jo raised her hand. 'What does being brave have to do with being the Ice Princess?' she asked. 'I thought she just had to do a dance.'

The headteacher's face grew serious. 'There is more to being the Ice Princess than you have been told, Jo. The dance takes place in a difficult spot and the journey there might be long . . . and even dangerous. For these reasons, the Ice Princess will need to be brave.'

The girls all held their breath as they waited for Madame Letsworth to go on, but she didn't explain further. 'You'll find out more in time,' she told them firmly. 'For now, doesn't anyone want to know what this week's winner will receive?'

'Oh, yes!' cried several voices. Issy sensed that some of the girls were relieved to change the subject, which she didn't understand at all. She was longing to hear more about where the Ice Princess would skate and the dangerous journey!

'These amber skates will be the prize for this week's winner,' Madame Letsworth said, holding up a pair of sparkling orange-yellow skates.

They were beautiful! Issy hoped she would win them.

'Like last week, you're to plan your routine yourselves and design your own costumes,' said Madame Letsworth. 'You may choose your own music as well.'

Issy felt fizzy with excitement. She could hardly wait to start planning her

routine. She knew exactly what she
wanted to do!

'Right, what do you think of this?'
said Issy eagerly. She and Sophy were
in the music room later that day, trying
out different pieces of music for their
routines. Issy had decided on a wild,
lively piece of music that made her
feel like laughing whenever she heard
it.

    'So, I'm going to start with a double
toe loop and then a double axel then a
Flying Camel. After that I'll do some
crossovers and then a double lutz–double
toe loop . . .' Issy demonstrated each
move as best she could as she spoke.
'And I'll end with another double axel!'
she finished, whirling up in the air.

But, without skating, she couldn't get the height she needed, and she stumbled and fell on to the carpet. She bounced up again, laughing as the ice dragons in the music box stood up and applauded.

Sophy looked doubtful. 'Two double axels? But you're still trying to learn them. Why don't you stick to the double lutz?'

'No way!' exclaimed Issy, pushing back her thick blonde hair. 'Madame Letsworth said to challenge ourselves, remember?'

Sophy laughed. 'Well, that will certainly be a challenge! OK, do you want to see mine?'

Sophy had selected a slow, sweetly sad piece of music. As the ice dragons began working the series of wheels and levers that made it play, she went to the centre of the room. 'Right, I thought I'd do some backward crossovers, a Flying Camel, and then more backward crossovers and a single lutz–single toe loop, and then a spiral . . .'

She demonstrated as Issy had done, leaping and spinning about the carpet. When she'd finished, she looked at Issy hopefully. 'What do you think?'

'Is that it?' Issy blurted out.

Sophy stared at her. 'What do you mean?'

Issy realized that she'd said the wrong thing. 'Nothing! It's a great routine. It's just . . . well, maybe you should push yourself more.'

'I *am* pushing myself,' said Sophy defensively.

'Really?'

'Yes!' Sophy insisted. 'Not everyone is as fearless as you, Issy!'

Issy blinked. 'Fearless? What are you talking about?'

Sophy crossed her arms over her chest. 'When's the last time you felt scared doing a jump?'

Issy shrugged. 'Well . . . never.'

'Exactly!' said Sophy as if that proved her point. 'Some people actually find jumps pretty scary, Issy.'

'I know that!' protested Issy. She felt a bit silly. 'It's just that –'

'Just that *you're* not one of them,' finished Sophy. She rolled her eyes good-naturedly. 'It's OK. I'm not mad at you. I'm just trying to explain that this routine *is* difficult for me.' She smiled. 'Come on, we can practise some more later. We'd better get to class!'

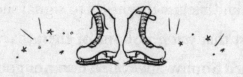

Chapter Three
Accident on the Ice

For the next two days, Issy practised her
routine over and over again. To her
delight, the double axel started to get
easier. It was such an amazing feeling to
leap so high and spin so quickly through
the air.

'Very good, Issy,' commented Madame
Letsworth when Issy had got the double
axel right twice in a row. 'You've made

real progress with that jump.' She turned away and blew her whistle to signal the end of the lesson. 'All right, girls, that's enough for now. We'll have an hour's break for lunch and then it's time for your ballet class.'

Sophy skated across to join Issy as they left the ice. 'You're doing great with your routine. I saw that last double axel – it was fantastic!'

'Thanks,' said Issy with a grin. She remembered their conversation from before and, though she understood what Sophy had been saying, she still privately thought Sophy could maybe push herself a bit more. Still, Issy didn't want to upset her so she smiled. 'You're doing great too. I hope one of us is going to win.'

As they changed out of their skates, Jo

came over. 'Hi, Is,' she said, ignoring
Sophy. 'Maisie, Milly and me are going to
go sledging. Do you want to come?'

'Yeah,' Issy said eagerly. 'You'll come
too, won't you, Sophy?' She saw Jo and
Sophy look at each other.

'I think I'll give it a miss,' said Sophy. 'I
want to go and see the frost fairies in my
dorm.'

'OK, you do that,' Jo said quickly, linking arms with Issy. 'Come on, Is. Let's go!'

It was fun sledging at lunchtime, but Issy kept thinking about Sophy and wishing she was there too. She caught up with her as they got changed into leotards and tights for their first afternoon class – a ballet lesson. Sophy seemed quiet and Issy had the feeling she was a bit upset. *She could have come sledging*, Issy told herself. But she still felt a bit bad.

In the ballet class, the girls all lined up at the long barre. Though Issy had done lots of gymnastics, she had never done ballet, and she found the moves difficult to get the hang of. Some of the other girls, like Milly and Jessica, had taken ballet for years and were very good at it, sweeping down

into their pliés and rising up on their toes
with their arms perfectly extended to the
side, their movements flowing and
smooth.

Madame Breshnev, their ballet teacher,
checked each girl's posture as she walked
past. 'Graceful lines, please!' she called.
'And rest.' She went down the room to the
music box.

As the girls relaxed, Cecilia, who
was a few girls in front of Issy, gazed at

herself in the mirror. 'Oh, gosh, I haven't got a spot, have I?' she murmured worriedly, touching her chin. 'Maybe the frost fairies can make me some spot cream . . .'

From behind her, Issy heard Jo sputter with laughter. 'You know what Cecilia should do to show she's brave enough to be the Ice Princess?' she hissed to Issy. 'She should go out in public with a hair out of place. Now that really *would* be brave!'

Issy giggled. Several other girls nearby had heard too. Sniggers floated around the classroom.

Cecilia had been so busy looking at her reflection that she hadn't caught the remark. She looked at the giggling girls, her face confused. 'What's up?'

Jo smirked. 'Oh, nothing.' Her eyes glinted. 'You'd better get some make-up on that spot though before you frighten the frost fairies!' She grinned round at the others as she spoke.

Cecilia flushed. Issy saw Sophy open her mouth, but before she could say anything

there was a bang as Madame Breshnev hit the floor with her stick.

'Pay attention, please, girls! Now, from the start. First position . . .'

After class, Sophy seemed in a bit of a mood, grumpily shoving her ballet things into her locker.

'What's up?' asked Issy.

Sophy made a face. 'Jo.' Glancing over her shoulder to make sure they were alone, she whispered, 'I just don't get why you're friends with her.'

'What do you mean?' said Issy in surprise.

'What do you think?' Sophy's hazel eyes flashed. 'She was really mean to Cecilia back in class. Making everyone laugh at her like that and saying those things about her spot!'

Issy's cheeks grew warm. Jo's comment had made her giggle along with some of the others. 'But I said something about Cecilia too, the other day,' she pointed out uncomfortably. 'What's the difference?'

Sophy looked exasperated. 'Because you didn't do it to make everyone laugh at her. Jo is always *getting* at people and I think it was a horrible thing to do. Afterwards Cecilia couldn't concentrate at all. I was watching her and she was really upset.'

Issy felt all hot and bothered. She couldn't help thinking Sophy was right and she did feel guilty now for laughing at Cecilia, but she also didn't want to be mean about Jo. 'She didn't say it to be horrible,' she said defensively.

Sophy raised her eyebrows and stared at Issy.

'Oh, you're taking it all too seriously!' Issy grabbed her things and headed for the door. 'I'm going to go skating.'

Sophy sighed, looking as if she already regretted the row. 'Issy . . .'

But Issy was already gone, banging the changing-room door behind her.

When Issy got on to the ice, she still felt upset and cross. She plunged into her routine like a whirlwind. No matter what problems she had, skating usually made her feel better. But right now it didn't seem to be working its magic.

She landed the first double axel badly, wobbling on her right leg and tumbling on

to the ice. She sighed as she got up. She
had managed it before! Suddenly it almost
seemed like it was Sophy's fault that the
jump was difficult again. Issy hated arguing
with people. Why had Sophy got in a
mood? Couldn't she see that Jo just liked
messing around?

Cecilia's hurt face flashed into Issy's
mind. *Maybe Sophy does have a point*, a
little voice at the back of her mind
said.

Issy slammed it away. *Just skate*, she told
herself. She zoomed about the ice, faster
and faster. She'd do the double axel again.
Ready . . . and . . . *now*!

Issy flung herself wildly into the air,
spinning like a top. Once . . . twice . . .
another half a rotation . . .

As she landed, Issy's feet shot out from
under her. Before she could scream, she hit
the ice . . . and then the world went black.

Chapter Four
Off the Ice

When Issy woke up, she was lying in a clean white bed in a large room with lots of other beds in it.

'Hello, my dear,' said an ice sylph with short grey hair and a kind, no-nonsense manner. She was the school's Matron. She poured Issy a glass of water. 'I'm glad to see you awake. That was a nasty fall you took!'

'I . . . I fell?' mumbled Issy. Then it all came back to her. Touching her head, she winced. It really hurt!

'You've got concussion,' explained Matron. 'The doctor says you'll be right as snow in a day or two. But for now, I'm afraid you're stuck in here. Don't worry, you'll still have time to practise for the

competition once you're better,' she added. 'I know that's all you girls think about.'

The competition! Somehow Issy had forgotten all about it. *Yes, of course*, she thought dazedly. She needed to practise.

'Would you like to see Sophy?' Matron asked with a smile. 'She's been waiting outside for hours.'

Sophy! Issy tried to sit up as their row came back to her. *Ouch!* Her head throbbed and she fell back against the pillows. 'Yes, please,' she said faintly.

Matron went off and a few minutes later Sophy came rushing in. 'Oh, Issy!' she cried, dropping into a chair beside Issy's bed. 'Are you OK? I've been so worried.'

Issy nodded. 'It's just concussion, Matron says. I'll be OK in a day or two.'

Sophy grinned in relief. 'That means

46

you'll still be able to be in the
competition.'

Issy pictured the double axel at the end
of her routine. She swallowed. 'Yeah, isn't
that great?' she said weakly.

'And Is, I'm *so* sorry about our row,'
Sophy went on quickly. 'I shouldn't have
said anything about Jo.'

'That's OK,' said Issy awkwardly. 'You
were right. Jo does get at people too much
sometimes. I shouldn't have stormed off
like that.'

Sophy looked uncomfortable. 'You only
did because she's your friend and I was
being horrid about her. I don't blame you.'
She took a deep breath. 'I – I suppose I'm
sort of jealous.'

Issy stared at her in surprise. 'Jealous?
What for?'

Sophy gave an embarrassed shrug. 'Well, you *do* have a lot in common with Jo, and – and the two of you are in the same dorm together, and –'

'Sophy, don't be daft!' cried Issy. 'I've got much more in common with you! No one else understands at all about how cool this land is.'

Sophy bit her lip, looking as if she wanted to believe Issy. 'Really?' she said.

'Really,' Issy assured her. 'You're my *best* friend, Sophy. Nothing can change that.'

Sophy's face cleared. 'Sorry,' she said sheepishly. 'I was being really stupid, wasn't I?'

'Yes!' said Issy firmly and they both laughed.

'Oh, I almost forgot!' cried Sophy. She opened her bag. 'I borrowed some books from Madame Longley for you to read, and Cobweb gave me some chocolate for you. And here's your toothbrush too.' She put the things on Issy's bedside table. 'Is there anything else you'd like?'

'No thanks, this is brilliant,' said Issy. Sophy was the best friend in the world!

Matron reappeared, striding briskly across the sick bay. 'I think that's probably enough time now, Sophy. Issy needs to rest.'

Sophy nodded. 'Bye,' she said, getting up. 'I'll see you tomorrow. I guess you'll be desperate to get on the ice as soon as possible to make up for missing today.'

'Yeah,' Issy said slowly. She waved as Sophy left. Then her smile faded as she thought again about practising for the competition. Issy realized she didn't want to. *What's wrong with me?* she thought in confusion.

Troubled, she picked up one of the books Sophy had left and tried to lose herself in the story. But although she stared at the words, all she could think about was the competition. She relived the moment where she had taken off into the air on her double axel, felt herself spinning, losing control . . .

No! Issy quickly stared at the book again.

The next morning the doctor said Issy could leave the sick bay, but that she wasn't ready to do anything too active yet. Issy felt a rush of relief when she heard that. *It is too early to get back on the ice*, she told herself. *It was a bad fall. He's right. I need some time to recover.*

Not sure what to do with herself, she wandered down to the rink while the others were having their lesson.

The three groups had all finished their footwork exercises and were now working on jumps and spins. The ice hummed with

activity as the girls whizzed past, hardly
noticing Issy as she stood in the shadows
on the wrong side of the silver barrier. She
shivered slightly as she watched them,
feeling strangely shut out from the bright,
busy world on the ice.

Milly picked up speed, her white skates a
blur. Suddenly she leapt into a double axel.
Issy caught her breath in alarm, not letting
it out again until Milly had landed
gracefully, gliding away across the ice.

Issy's heart thudded wildly. *I . . . I must
still be a bit woozy*, she thought. Maybe
coming down here hadn't been such a great
idea.

As she started to turn away, there was a
hiss of blades nearby. 'Hey there!' said Jo
cheerfully, pausing at the barrier. 'You're
out of the sick bay then. How are you?'

'Fine,' said Issy, trying to smile.

Jo cocked her head to one side as she regarded her. 'You look like you need cheering up, Is.' A gleam came into her light-brown eyes. 'And guess what? I think I've got just the thing!'

'What?' asked Issy in surprise. She hadn't really expected Jo to notice that she was feeling down.

'I'm not going to tell you yet,' said Jo with a grin. 'But it's going to be *amazing*, I promise!' Madame Li called to Jo then and she skated off, calling over her shoulder, 'Just wait and see!'

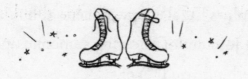

Chapter Five
Jo's Idea

That night at supper Jo kept raising her
eyebrows at Issy, giving her looks that said,
We've got a secret. Issy felt a tingle of
excitement as she remembered Jo's
promise.

Sophy noticed too. 'What's up with you
and Jo?' she whispered.

'I don't know,' confessed Issy. 'She says
she's going to do something to cheer me

up, but she won't say what it is yet.'

Sophy's hazel eyes widened. 'Oh . . . I hope Jo's idea of cheering someone up is something you'll like!'

Issy giggled. 'I'm sure she wouldn't do anything *too* bad,' she said.

Sophy started to say something else, but broke off as Vanessa's snooty voice rose above the chatter at their end of the table.

'Your twin seems to have found a new best friend, Maisie,' she said with a smirk. 'What's the matter – aren't you two speaking to each other?' She nudged Lou, who sniggered.

Issy looked at Vanessa with dislike. The blonde girl was always stirring and loved it when friends fell out with each other.

Maisie, who had been talking to Jo, looked up in surprise. 'What are you on about?' she asked.

'Well, she and Jessica seem awfully cosy now, don't they?' said Vanessa, pointing to the other end of the table. Milly and Jessica – a tall, slim girl who was as graceful on the ice as Milly was – were talking and laughing together.

Maisie shook her head. 'So what? We're

just twins – we're not joined at the hip!
We're allowed to have other friends. And
Milly and Jess have loads in common.'

Vanessa looked flustered. She tossed her
head, trying to hide it. 'Well – I just
thought –'

'*Don't* think, OK?' broke in Maisie. 'You
don't seem to be very good at it!' Suddenly
her eyes sparkled and she broke into song.
'*Act your age, not your shoe size!*' she warbled
at Vanessa.

The girls around them all burst into
laughter. 'Very mature!' sniffed Vanessa,
turning away.

To Issy's relief, Sophy didn't say
anything else about Jo after that. Instead
the two girls talked about the baby ice
dragons in the woods, and whether they
might be trying to fly yet. But, as Jo gave

her a secret wink, Issy felt a nervous excitement flutter through her.

What *was* Jo up to?

On Friday Issy was allowed back on to the ice. She changed out of her slipper-boots in the changing room, fiddling for a long time with her skates.

'Aren't you coming?' asked Sophy, waiting for her.

Issy forced a smile. 'Yep, I'm just coming now.' Her heart was thumping as she and Sophy went to the rink together. *What's wrong with me?* she thought in confusion. *Why aren't I looking forward to skating?*

'It's lovely to have you back, Issy,' said Madame Letsworth with a warm smile as the other girls in the advanced group grinned at her. 'We're just about to practise our footwork exercises.'

For a change, Issy was glad to spend time on her footwork. The familiar exercises seemed comforting somehow. She felt herself begin to relax. But then it was time to work on their jumps. Madame Letsworth told Issy, Maisie and Jessica to practise their competition routines on their

own for a bit, while she helped Milly work on her triple toe loop.

Issy hesitated and then slowly started to skate. *I can do it*, she thought. *I'm just a bit out of practice after a few days off, that's all.* Taking a deep breath, she picked up speed. She managed the double toe loop fine. *OK*, she thought, taking another deep breath. *I can do this.*

Her first double axel was coming up. Getting ready, Issy leant on the forward outside edge of her right foot. Suddenly she remembered the terrifying sensation of her feet shooting out from under her. Her heart started pounding and she slowed back down, her feet still firmly on the ice.

She tried a second time, skating even faster. But it happened again. When Issy got to the point where she was supposed to jump, the fall flashed through her mind and she just couldn't bring herself to do it.

Issy felt a bit panicked. Quickly she went into backward crossovers, picking up speed. Shifting her weight to her left foot, she touched her right toe pick to the ice and leapt up into the air, spinning twice before she landed. Another double toe loop. At least she could do those.

Feeling better, she attempted a double axel again, but the same thing happened as before. Her body just seemed to freeze suddenly and she pulled sharply out of the jump, her heart thumping.

Madame Letsworth came gliding over to her. 'How are you doing, Issy?'

From her concerned tone, Issy knew

Madame Letsworth had noticed the way she had abandoned the double axel. 'Fine,' she said, looking down.

Madame Letsworth put a finger under Issy's chin, tipping her head up. 'My dear, there's nothing wrong with being afraid,' she said gently. 'Particularly after a bad fall. You must be able to confront fear to be a good skater . . . and to be the Ice Princess.'

'I'm not afraid,' Issy said quickly. She couldn't be; she had never been afraid of skating in her life!

Madame Letsworth looked at her steadily. 'I can see you've lost confidence. I wish I could tell you how to get it back, but everyone has to find their own way. You can do it, Issy, I promise you, but first you must admit it.'

Issy tried to smile. 'Thank you, but, um . . . I'm fine,' she said. 'I'm really not scared. I've . . . I've just still got a headache, I think, that's all. Please may I go inside now?'

Madame Letsworth gave her another long, level look and Issy felt her cheeks grow warm. 'Of course,' her teacher said finally. 'But, Issy, please think about what I've said, won't you?'

'I will,' said Issy. And then she skated off the ice as fast as she could.

'I've been looking everywhere for you!' exclaimed Sophy. Issy was in the library, reading a book about the different creatures that lived in the land. 'What happened to you during the lesson?'

'Nothing. I had a headache, that's all.' Issy turned a page guiltily.

Sophy sat down beside her, looking

concerned. 'Oh. Well . . . are you OK now?'

Issy shrugged. 'I suppose.'

'Do you think you'll be skating this afternoon, during free time?' asked Sophy.

Issy swallowed. Closing the book, she pushed it away. 'Maybe,' she said. 'But I've been thinking about my routine and – and I think you were right about the double axel all along. It's too difficult for me.'

Sophy's eyes widened. 'But you were doing really well with it. And what about pushing yourself, like you were saying I should do?'

Issy ran a finger over the book's cover. 'I know, but . . .' She trailed off.

Suddenly a look of understanding crossed Sophy's face. 'Is, are you scared of doing the double axel now?'

Issy felt irritation prickle through her. Why did everyone keep saying she was afraid? First Madame Letsworth and now Sophy . . .

'Of course not,' she said abruptly. 'I just don't see the point of working too hard this week, that's all. I've already missed so much practice that there's no way I'd win the competition anyway.'

Sophy stared at her. 'But that's not like you! You mean you're not even going to *try* the double axel again?'

Issy shook her head, feeling uncomfortable. 'No.'

'But what about being the Ice Princess, Is?' burst out Sophy. 'If you don't do a routine that shows courage then the teachers might not think about choosing you!'

'I don't care!' cried Issy. 'I don't really want to be the Ice Princess anyway.'

She felt her eyes get hot and she shoved her chair back and walked quickly away. She knew it was a lie about not wanting to be the Ice Princess, but she also knew she just couldn't do the double axel again, however hard she tried.

I can't, Issy thought despairingly. *I really can't.*

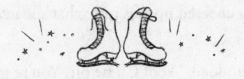

Chapter Six
The Prank

Issy went to bed that night feeling very unhappy. Though she'd apologized to Sophy soon after their row, the things that had been said still bothered her. Issy tried hard to go to sleep – she didn't want to think about it any more.

But then, the next morning, Issy was shaken awake by Jo. 'Are you ready?' she asked in a low voice, her eyes dancing.

Issy sat up in bed. 'Is it the surprise?' Being cheered up was just what she needed right now.

Jo nodded. 'Yep! Come on. You're going to *love* this!' She crept towards the Ice Owls door. Issy followed. What had Jo done?

Maisie woke up. 'Where are you two going so early?' she asked drowsily.

Jo grinned at her. 'We're not going anywhere . . . yet. We're just going to wait.' Motioning for Issy to join her, she opened the door a crack and peered out into the corridor. Milly woke up too and exchanged a confused look with her twin.

'Jo, what –' she started to ask.

'Shush!' Jo waved a hand at her. She seemed to be listening hard. 'I think . . . yes . . . this is it!'

Maisie and Milly leapt out of bed, joining them at the doorway. 'This is *what*?' demanded Maisie.

'Just listen!' laughed Jo.

Craning to hear, Issy thought she heard a faint screeching noise from the Snow Foxes dorm. 'What *is* that?' she asked, her eyes wide.

'It sounds like it's coming from the

washroom,' said Milly in confusion. 'Jo, what's going on?'

Jo giggled. 'I think we can go and see now,' she said. 'Come on!' Throwing open the door, she raced down the corridor with the other girls following. Issy was beginning to feel a bit alarmed. What had Jo done?

The screams got louder and louder. As they reached the Snow Foxes dorm, the washroom door burst open.

'My HAIR!' somebody shrieked. 'OH, NO, LOOK AT MY HAAIIRRR!!!'

'Is that *Cecilia*?' gasped Milly as all the other Snow Foxes ran out of their dorm to see what was going on.

Cecilia burst out of the washroom in her dressing gown, dripping wet as if she'd just had a shower. And her hair was . . . bright green!

Issy clutched Jo's arm. 'Jo!' she hissed. 'You didn't –'

'MY HAIR! LOOK AT MY HAIR!' Cecilia howled at them. 'IT'S GREEEEENN!!'

Jo, Maisie and a few of the other girls collapsed into laughter, holding on to the wall to support themselves. Issy felt too stunned to laugh. The sight of Cecilia with bright-green hair was quite shocking.

'It's not funny, you lot!' shouted Cecilia, stamping her foot. She looked close to tears. 'Look at my hair! It's GREEN!'

'We're looking, we're looking!' gasped Jo in between laughs.

'How can I skate with green hair?' wailed Cecilia. 'The competition's tomorrow!' She burst into noisy tears, covering her face with her hands.

Sophy dashed forward and put an arm round her. 'Come on, let's get you to Matron,' she soothed. 'I bet she can sort you out!'

Sophy gave Jo a furious look as she led the sobbing Cecilia down the corridor. Issy knew Sophy was thinking that she had been right all along about Jo. She bit her lip. Seeing Cecilia's green hair had been pretty funny . . . but seeing Cecilia so upset wasn't funny at all.

Once Cecilia was gone, the girls burst into excited conversation. 'Jo, I bet *you* know something about this,' said another girl from Snow Foxes, Jessica, putting her hands on her hips.

'Who, me?' said Jo innocently.

Back in the Ice Owls dorm, Jo confessed: she had put crushed-up rainbow berries, which they had learnt about in Madame Longley's class that week, in Cecilia's shampoo.

'It took me *ages* to find the berries,' said Jo. 'And isn't it lucky that they were green this week? That's just the colour I would have chosen!'

Maisie shook her head with a grin. 'You're terrible, Jo,' she said. 'But I have to admit, that was one of the funniest things I've ever seen!'

Milly didn't look so convinced. 'Well, maybe this will teach Cecilia not to be so silly about her looks,' she shrugged.

Jo turned to Issy. 'What did *you* think?' she said eagerly. 'Are you feeling cheered up?'

Issy hesitated. She didn't want to upset Jo, but it had been a bit of a mean trick. 'Er, thanks for thinking of me, but I – I'm not sure you should have done it, Jo,' she said slowly. 'Cecilia was really upset.'

Jo's jaw dropped. 'What?' she spluttered. 'Who cares? It serves her right for being so vain! Besides, I'm sure the teachers will be able to fix it with their magic.'

Issy shook her head. 'I know, but . . .'

'Oh, honestly!' burst out Jo. 'You used to be fun, but since you started hanging out with Sophy, you've become really boring!'

'Be quiet!' Issy snapped. 'Sophy's my friend. Stop being mean about her. If you can't then we can't be friends any more!'

To Issy's surprise, Jo didn't laugh or make a snide comment. She gaped at Issy for a moment then shrugged stiffly and turned away.

'Fine. Whatever,' she said.

Maisie and Milly began to chat awkwardly, changing the subject. Issy let out a breath. It hadn't been easy standing up to Jo and she doubted she would have done it if everything else hadn't been going on. She just hoped it had been worth it.

Cecilia was late to breakfast that morning. When she finally arrived, every girl in the hall stopped eating to look at her.

Cecilia's hair was mostly chestnut again, Issy saw with relief, although it still had a few faint streaks of green here and there. She was wearing it pulled up in a jaunty ponytail and she had even stuck a pink snow flower behind one ear.

Though her eyes were still puffy from

crying, Cecilia sat down with her chin held high as if nothing had happened. 'Hi,' she said to everyone.

Issy felt a flash of admiration for her. She wasn't sure whether she could have faced everyone again so coolly, after something like that.

Jo seemed to feel the same way. She bit her lip and then said, 'Um, Cecilia . . . is your hair going to be OK?'

Cecilia nodded. 'Matron put a special solution on it. She said that what's left should have faded by the competition.'

'That's good,' said Jo. She cleared her throat. Her face was bright pink. 'And, um . . . you know, it was probably just meant to be a joke, Cecilia. I mean . . . whoever did it, they – they probably didn't mean anything by it really.'

Issy was surprised. Even though she hadn't actually said the word 'sorry', Issy knew this was probably as close to an apology as Jo would ever come.

Cecilia gave Jo a look that said she knew exactly who had put the dye in her shampoo! Finally she shrugged her shoulders. 'That's OK,' she said. 'I suppose it *was* pretty funny. Me having green hair!' She giggled.

Everyone else at the table laughed too – but this time it was with Cecilia, not at her.

As they all went back to talking and eating their breakfast, Issy whispered to Sophy, 'I can't believe that she actually laughed about it! Wasn't she brilliant?'

Sophy nodded. 'I keep telling you – she's not bad at all. The only thing wrong with her is that she's always been told how pretty she is. She's really OK, apart from that. I bet coming in here with her hair like that was the worst thing she could imagine, but she did it anyway. She *tried*.'

Issy shot her friend a suspicious glance. Was Sophy trying to tell her something? 'That's true,' she said. 'But I've already told you . . . *I'm* not scared.'

Sophy shrugged and took a sip of her juice. 'I didn't say you were.'

Issy started to say something else and then stopped, her thoughts swirling about like snowflakes in a storm. *Was* she scared? She played with the rest of her breakfast, not feeling very hungry any more.

During her skating lesson that morning, Issy thought hard about what Sophy had said. *It's true*, she realized miserably. She might deny it, but if she was honest, she *was* afraid. With any of her other jumps, she was fine. But at the thought of doing a double axel, the memory of her fall came rushing back.

What am I going to do? she thought in despair. The competition was tomorrow. How could she show courage to the judges when she couldn't even do the jump?

Issy gazed at the snowy land around her. It sparkled and shone as if it had been coated with diamond dust. She hated the thought of it being in danger! And the only way she could help it was by trying as hard as she could to be the Ice Princess.

Issy took a deep breath. *I'm going to try the double axel again*, she decided. *I have to, whether I'm scared or not!* Then she looked around at the busy rink and bit her lip. *Only . . . not now, with everyone watching*, she thought. *I'll do it on my own tonight.*

Chapter Seven
Sophy's Surprise

That night, when everyone was asleep, Issy sneaked down to the rink. The lights came on automatically the moment she stepped on to the ice. With a surprised rustle, the ice dragons popped their heads over the side of the music box inquisitively.

Issy skated over to them. 'Hi,' she said. 'I'm sorry it's so late, but would you play my competition music for me, so I can practise?'

The ice dragons chirruped at her. They
began turning wheels and working levers
and a moment later Issy's music began. She
made a face at how light-hearted it was. It
wasn't at all the mood that she was in any
more.

Quickly Issy did her warm-up stretches.
Her heart pounded hard as she began her
routine, stroking her blades across the ice
and picking up speed. Her first jump was

the double axel. She waited for the beat in the music. *Now!* she thought.

Just as before, something inside Issy seemed to go cold and her feet stayed on the ice. She slowed down, her hands feeling clammy. She wiped them on her skirt and took a deep breath. OK, so she hadn't done it that time. No big deal. She'd just try again. But the same thing happened the next time, and the time after that. Over and over, Issy tried the jump, only to stop herself at the last moment. She just couldn't bring herself to do it.

After almost an hour, Issy felt close to tears. It was hopeless! Maybe she'd never be able to do a double axel again. Finally, discouraged, she skated across to the music box.

'Thanks,' she said. 'I . . . I suppose I'll go back to bed now.'

The ice dragons chirruped in concern. With a flutter of wings, they hovered above the box, gazing worriedly into Issy's eyes. She tried to smile. 'I'm fine,' she assured the little creatures. 'I'm just tired, that's all.'

As she skated off the rink, Issy sighed. She had woken up the poor ice dragons for nothing. The competition was tomorrow . . . and she was still no closer to doing the jump than before. What was she going to do?

The next day, the other girls in the Ice Owls dorm woke up with squeals of delight. Their costumes for the competition had arrived, delivered during the night by the frost fairies.

But Issy gazed glumly at hers. She had designed a bright-blue skating dress with jewels sparkling across the bodice, and lighter-blue feathers at the skirt and sleeves, like a bluebird. It had seemed so pretty when she first drew it . . . but now all she could think of was how much she was dreading the competition.

'Look at me!' exclaimed Maisie,

whirling about the room, holding a dark-red dress.

Milly's dress was a beautiful bright yellow and Jo's was bright pink with fluttery sleeves. Jo smiled across at Issy. 'Nice dress.'

'Thanks,' said Issy, smiling back. 'So's yours.' *At least we're friends again now*, thought Issy, *even though I stuck up for Sophy*. She was glad that she had been brave enough to do it.

She sighed, fiddling with one of the feathers on her dress. She knew she should go back on to the rink and practise some more before the competition that afternoon, but she couldn't bear to. It was bad enough being afraid to try the double axel when she was on her own; the last thing she needed was everyone watching her!

★

After breakfast that morning, Sophy gave Issy a long look and then pulled on her arm. 'Come on,' she said. 'I think we need to go somewhere!'

Issy looked at her in surprise. The other girls were on their way to the changing room, chattering excitedly about the competition that afternoon. 'Don't you want to practise with the others?' she asked.

Sophy shook her head firmly. 'Nope. I've had enough of practising for now, and so have you. You look like you need some cheering up and I've got a great idea for it!'

Issy hid a smile as she remembered Jo saying almost the exact same thing. Somehow she had a feeling that Sophy's idea of cheering her up was going to be very different!

'OK,' she said eagerly, relieved not to have to worry about her jump for a while. 'Where are we going?'

Sophy's hazel eyes flashed mysteriously. 'Follow me!' she said.

The two girls got dressed in warm jackets, scarves and boots. Soon they were walking through the woods, their feet crunching over the snow. Issy leant her head back and

breathed in deeply, smelling the sharp tang of pine.

'This is great,' she said happily. 'You were right, Sophy . . . it's just what I needed.'

Sophy laughed. 'Hey, we're not even there yet!' she teased. The girls walked a bit more, climbing over a snow-covered fallen log. When they came to a bend in the path, Sophy got behind Issy and put her mittened hands over Issy's eyes.

'OK, ready?' she said. 'Forward!'

Giggling, Issy took a few stumbling steps, guided by Sophy. They went around the bend and Issy's eyes widened behind the mittens. What was that flapping, squeaking noise? It sounded like . . .

Sophy took her mittens away. 'Ta-da!' she whispered.

'*Oh!*' breathed Issy. Fluttering in front of them were half a dozen baby ice dragons! Their nests were in the trees above and they were tumbling about in the air, beating their wings wildly as they learnt how to fly.

Issy laughed out loud as she watched them. They were the cutest things she'd ever seen! One of them, no bigger than her little finger, landed at her feet, panting for breath.

'Hi,' whispered Issy, kneeling down and stroking his pale-blue back. He blinked with pleasure, blowing ice crystals from his nostrils.

His mother appeared, swooping down and picking him up. Taking him back up to the nest again, she placed him on its edge. Issy watched as he paused for a moment, looking nervous – and then he jumped! His wings flapped wildly as he tossed and turned in the air. The little dragon landed in a heap in the snow, but as soon as his mum picked him up and put him back in the nest, he tried again. And then again and again, until he managed to fly right round the tree!

Looking delighted with himself, the baby dragon landed back in the nest. Issy was so pleased, she felt like clapping him, but she didn't want to scare him or the others.

The girls watched the ice dragons for ages, laughing at their antics. Finally they sensed that the mother dragons were becoming restless at having them there and they stole quietly away.

'Sophy, thanks *so* much,' said Issy, squeezing her friend's arm. 'That was the best surprise ever.'

Sophy grinned at her. 'I had a feeling you might like it!'

But as the turrets of the school came back into view, Issy's high spirits faded. Seeing the baby ice dragons had been wonderful . . . but she still had to perform in the competition that afternoon. She shivered.

'What's wrong?' asked Sophy.

Issy took a deep breath. 'It's just . . . well, you were right,' she confessed. 'I'm scared of doing double axels now. And I've tried so hard!' She described how she had sneaked down to the skating rink the night before. 'I'm so afraid of falling again that I freeze up,' she finished sadly. 'I get to the jump and I just can't do it.'

'But Issy, that happens to everyone sometimes!' exclaimed Sophy.

Issy felt like crying. She wiped her eyes with her mitten. 'Well, it's never happened to *me* before. I don't know what to do. Even Madame Letsworth said she couldn't help me, that I had to do it myself. Well, I can't. I'm hopeless.'

Sophy stopped and faced her. 'You're *not* hopeless,' she said firmly. 'You just have to keep at it!'

Issy sighed. She knew that Sophy was trying to make her feel better, but she had tried so many times already! 'Anyway, I suppose it doesn't matter how I do,' Issy said sadly. 'I obviously don't have what it takes to be the Ice Princess after all. She has to be brave and I'm *so* not.'

Sophy gave her a friendly nudge. 'Don't be daft! My dad always says that being brave doesn't mean *not* being scared. It means being scared, but doing something anyway.'

Issy's forehead creased. It was kind of Sophy to try and cheer her up, but how could you be afraid and brave at the same time? It didn't make any sense!

She could hear the other girls practising their routines in the distance. 'Come on, we'd better get back,' Issy said reluctantly. 'The competition will be starting soon.'

Chapter Eight
The Amber Skates

Half an hour before the competition, the changing room was busy with girls getting dressed and doing their hair. Gazing in the mirror, Issy put on a little bit of make-up, which they were allowed to wear for competitions. First pulling her thick blonde hair into a ponytail, she put on blue eyeshadow, lipgloss and mascara, and

then stroked silvery glitter on to her
cheekbones.

Finally she pulled on her bright-blue
costume. She *did* look nice, she thought.
If only she wasn't so scared! Biting her
lip nervously, Issy laced up her skates
and then tied a blue scarf round her
ponytail. When she had first planned her
costume, she had imagined the scarf
fluttering behind her like a bird's wings.
Now all she could think of was it

hanging limply from her hair as she froze on her double axel!

'Aargh!' shrieked Jo suddenly. She jumped up from her bench, shaking out her skate. Water and slushy snow dripped from it. 'There's – there's a *snowball* in my skate!' she spluttered in disbelief.

'Gosh, I wonder how that got in there,' said Cecilia innocently. Her eyes sparkled.

Everyone stared at her for a moment and then started howling with laughter – Jo loudest of all! 'Good one, Cecilia' she said with a grin. 'You got me.'

Despite her worries, Issy smiled at Jo, glad she had taken the joke in good spirits.

The frost fairies zoomed forward, quickly drying Jo's skate for her. Then it was time. The girls headed out towards the ice. Sophy squeezed Issy's hand. 'Good luck!' she whispered.

'Thanks,' Issy whispered back. *I'm going to need it*, she thought glumly.

Issy waited nervously by the edge of the rink as the competition started. As last week, the judges were the three skating teachers. They sat behind a big table while other ice sylphs watched from the seats round the rink.

Only it's not like last week at all, thought Issy. She had actually been *excited* about performing then. It seemed hard to believe now. She swallowed hard and wiped her damp palms on her skirt.

Maisie was first on the ice. She glided out and took up her position. As the music started, she flung herself into a very showy routine with lots of spins and jumps, all performed dead on time with the beats of the music. Everyone clapped loudly as she finished. Cecilia was next, dancing a surprisingly tricky-looking routine. *She's really improved*, thought Issy, watching her. Jo went after Cecilia. She barrelled around the ice like a dynamo, doing lots of high-speed jumps and turns. She fell over three times and lost her way once, but didn't seem to mind.

After each girl finished, the teachers consulted for a moment and then the frost

fairies shot up into the air, forming the numbers of each girl's score. So far, Maisie was in the lead, with Cecilia second and Abigail from the Frost Fairies dorm third. Issy licked her lips nervously as it got closer and closer to her turn.

Glancing at the ice dragons in their music box, she thought wistfully about how lovely it had been out in the woods that morning with Sophy. The baby ice dragons had been so cute! She smiled as she remembered how nervous the one who landed at her feet had been, and then how he had flung himself into the air anyway.

Suddenly a shock went through Issy as something clicked into place. That's exactly what Sophy had been trying to tell her! You *could* be brave even though you were scared. The important thing was

trying, whether you were frightened or
not . . . just like the baby ice dragon had.

'Issy! It's your turn!' whispered Sophy,
shaking her arm. Issy's heart was thumping
as she skated out on to the ice. *I'm scared,
but I'm going to do it anyway*, she thought,
lifting her arms into position. *If I fall, I fall
. . . but I've got to try!*

The music started. Issy took a deep
breath and began. To her surprise, she
found herself getting into the music as she
did her first spin and then picked up speed.
Coming to her first double axel, she didn't
give herself time to even think about her
fear. She just put her weight on her left
outside blade and jumped, spinning in the
air.

Issy was so surprised to find herself
actually doing the double axel that her

foot wobbled as she landed and she went
sprawling! She jumped back up again, joy
rushing through her. She had done it! Even
the fact that she'd fallen again seemed OK.
She hadn't hurt herself at all!

With a big grin on her face, Issy went
through the rest of her routine. Stepping
with her left foot into a Flying Camel, as
she spun round faster and faster, she lifted
her right leg up and pulled her arms back
along her body. She felt wonderful – as if
she owned the ice. Starting to skate
backwards again, she prepared herself for
her next jump.

As the happy music reached its climax
and Issy came to her second and final
double axel, she threw herself into it with
no hesitation. She wobbled again as she
landed, but didn't fall this time. *Yes!* she

thought, only just stopping herself from punching the air.

She finished her routine, throwing her arms back on the beat. The ice sylphs applauded and she saw Madame Letsworth smiling at her. Issy's own smile was huge as she skated back to the barrier.

'You did it! You did the double axel!' squealed Sophy.

'Well, you did wobble a lot on it,' said Vanessa unkindly.

Issy ignored her. She might have wobbled, but she was just too thrilled to care. She had done the jump as she had planned – that was all that mattered!

Jo gasped and pointed to the frost fairies. 'Look! You're in the lead, Issy!' She hugged her. 'That's brilliant!'

To Issy's amazement, it was true. She was first now. By the time the other girls had finished, Jessica had taken over from Cecilia in third place . . . but Issy was still the winner.

'I can't believe it!' she gasped. The girls crowded round, congratulating her. At the judges' table, Madame Letsworth stood up and motioned for silence.

'Well done, everyone,' she said. 'You've

all worked hard this week and it shows!
You were judged on two things today:
accuracy and your bravery in pushing
yourself. Our winner this week is Issy
who, as you all know, took a bad fall
when doing a double axel earlier this
week. Unsurprisingly she was then
extremely nervous about trying that jump
again.'

She paused for a moment and silence fell
across the rink. Issy felt her ears turn hot
with embarrassment as Madame Letsworth
went on.

'This sort of fear is something that all
skaters have to deal with at some point and
it takes a lot of courage to overcome it. So,
without a doubt, our winner this week is
Issy. Well done, Issy. Come and get your
prize!'

In a daze, Issy stepped back on to the ice
and skated over to the table. She could
hear her friends cheering as Madame
Letsworth handed her a glittering pair of
skates that were decorated with rich amber
jewels.

'Thank you!' she gasped.

Madame Letsworth squeezed her shoulder. 'I told you that you'd have to find your own way, Issy, and you've done it very well. I'm proud of you.'

Issy skated back to her friends, her heart light. Perhaps Madame Letsworth was right and she had found her own way . . . but she knew that she could never have done so without Sophy's help. And the baby ice dragon, of course! She grinned as she thought of him.

The girls all crowded around her, exclaiming over her skates as she stepped back through the barrier.

'Can I borrow them sometime?' Jo asked.

'Of course,' said Issy, smiling at her.

As everyone started drifting off to get

changed, Issy and Sophy exchanged a
smile. 'I wonder what next week's
competition will be?' said Sophy.

Issy shook her head. 'I don't know,'
she said. 'But I can hardly wait to find
out!'

She gazed down at her sparkling honey-
coloured skates. She could still hardly
believe it. She had been so afraid, but she
had tried anyway . . . and it had been the
best feeling in the world!

And this is the best school *in the world*,
Issy thought happily. 'Come on,' she
said to Sophy. 'Let's get changed and see
if the others want to have a snowball
fight!'

Sophy giggled. 'Better not mention
snowballs to Jo!'

Linking arms, the two friends headed

towards the changing room. *Another week over*, thought Issy. And the next week would bring even more adventure. She couldn't wait!

Do you dream of becoming an Ice Princess?

Have you ever wanted to go to a REAL Skating School?

All readers of *Skating School* get FREE membership to the National Ice Skating Association's Skate UK programme!

Skate UK will help you to learn all the moves and basic skills you need to become a true Ice Princess! It's all about fun and continuous movement and is taught in groups, so why not share your love of *Skating School* with your friends and bring them too?

To get your free membership, go to
www.iceskating.org.uk/skatingschool
and enter the secret password: **Twirl**.

Skate UK is taught by licensed NISA coaches and can be assisted by trained Programme Assistants.

For full terms and conditions visit:
www.lindachapman.co.uk
www.iceskating.org.uk/skatingschool

Do you want to enter super competitions,
get sneak previews and download lots of
Skating School fun?

Get YOUR skates on
join the
Sparkle Club
today!
lindachapman.co.uk

Just enter this secret password:

Twirl

The Land of Ice and Winter is waiting for you ...

Design your own ice-skating dress!

The tiny frost fairies have been working overtime designing the beautiful dresses for the girls to wear in the Ice-skating Academy competitions.

Using this dress as a template, the fairies need you to draw the most magical ice-skating outfit you can think of. Every month one lucky winner will receive a magical *Skating School* goody bag!

Send your drawing

with your name and address to:

Skating School Competition, Puffin Marketing, 80 Strand, London WC2R 0RL

Or e-mail them to: **skatingschool@uk.penguingroup.com**

Welcome to the magical Land of Ice and Winter
… a world where all your dreams come true!

Join in the magic with Emily and
her friends in the very first
Skating School series

Hi there,

I hope you've enjoyed reading about the adventures of the girls who go to the Magic Ice-skating Academy. I love writing them all down! Wouldn't it be amazing to go to the Land of Ice and Winter and see all the creatures who live there? Can you imagine holding an actual ice dragon or talking to a frost fairy?

Sometimes readers write to me and ask about my life. Being a writer is the best job ever. I live in a cottage in a village with my family and two dogs – a Bernese mountain dog and a golden retriever. I spend my days writing and going to visit schools and libraries to talk about writing.

I always think I'm really lucky because I get to spend my days writing about magic – mermaids, unicorns, stardust spirits, genies and now the Land of Ice and Winter. If you love them too then why not go to **www.lindachapman.co.uk** and join the Sparkle Club? It's my online fan club with loads of activities and downloads, and you can only get to it by using the secret password at the back of this book. Have fun!

Love,

Linda
xxx

It all started with a Scarecrow.

Puffin is seventy years old.
Sounds ancient, doesn't it? But Puffin has never been
so lively. We're always on the lookout for the next big
idea, which is how it began all those years ago.

Penguin Books was a big idea from the mind of
a man called Allen Lane, who in 1935 invented
the quality paperback and changed the world.
**And from great Penguins, great Puffins grew,
changing the face of children's books forever.**

The first four Puffin Picture Books were hatched in 1940 and the
first Puffin story book featured a man with broomstick arms called
Worzel Gummidge. In 1967 Kaye Webb, Puffin Editor, started the
Puffin Club, promising to **'make children into readers'**.
She kept that promise and over 200,000 children became
devoted Puffineers through their quarterly instalments of
Puffin Post, which is now back for a new generation.

Many years from now, we hope you'll look back and
remember Puffin with a smile. **No matter what your age
or what you're into, there's a Puffin for everyone.**
The possibilities are endless, but one thing is for sure:
whether it's a picture book or a paperback, a sticker book
or a hardback, **if it's got that little Puffin
on it – it's bound to be good.**